Marie-Claire
DARK
SPRING

KATHY STINSON

MARIE-CLAIRE

DARK
SPRING

KATHY STINSON

Penguin Books

PENGUIN BOOKS

Published by the Penguin Group

Penguin Books Canada Ltd, 10 Alcorn Avenue, Toronto, Ontario,
Canada M4V 3B2

Penguin Books Ltd, 27 Wrights Lane, London W8 5TZ, England

Penguin Putnam Inc., 375 Hudson Street, New York, New York 10014, U.S.A

Penguin Books Australia Ltd, Ringwood, Victoria, Australia

Penguin Books (NZ) Ltd, cnr Rosedale and Airborne Roads, Albany,
Auckland 1310, New Zealand

Penguin Books Ltd, Registered Offices: Harmondsworth, Middlesex, England

DESIGN: MATTHEWS COMMUNICATIONS DESIGN INC.

MAP ILLUSTRATION: SHARON MATTHEWS

INTERIOR ILLUSTRATIONS: SHARIF TARABAY

First published, 2001

1   3   5   7   9   10   8   6   4   2

Copyright © Kathy Stinson, 2001

Manufactured in Canada

NATIONAL LIBRARY OF CANADA CATALOGUING IN PUBLICATION DATA

Stinson, Kathy

Dark spring : Marie-Claire

(Our Canadian girl)

ISBN 0-14-100328-6

I. Title. II. Series.

PS8587.T56D37 2001   jC813'.54 C2001-901158-X

PZ7.S852Da 2001

Visit Penguin Canada's website at **www.penguin.ca**

MEET MARIE-CLAIRE

MARIE-CLAIRE IS A FRENCH-CANADIAN GIRL living in Montreal.

In 1885, when Marie-Claire is ten years old, Montreal is one of the filthiest cities in North America. Garbage is not collected regularly. Untreated sewage contaminates the river and even the streets. Smoke from the growing number of factories pollutes the air. The stench of it all, especially during warm weather, is downright disgusting.

The adults in Marie-Claire's life understand that filth is in some way partly responsible for people getting sick so often, but the building of water and sewage systems cannot keep up with the needs of the city's rapidly growing population.

Many people, attracted by business opportunities and jobs for unskilled workers, have been coming to Montreal from England, Scotland, Ireland, and from the Quebec countryside. Anglophones tend to settle in the west end of the city, francophones in the east.

Living conditions are worst for people like Marie-Claire's family, the working class which makes up the majority of Montreal's population. They cannot afford the fine stone homes at the base of the mountain. That's where business owners, bankers, doctors, and lawyers live. Marie-Claire's family lives closer to the river, where homes made of wood are crowded closely together and have no indoor plumbing—conditions ideal for the spread of disease. Diphtheria, cholera, tuberculosis, and smallpox have all visited the city in recent years.

Religion is an important part of most people's lives, including children like Marie-Claire. This is reflected in the way the steeples of Montreal's many fine churches stand out prominently against the city's skyline.

Wages are low, however, and working conditions unsafe. Taking care of a home and family is hard work. Both parents, and sometimes children, work long hours, six days a week. If even one parent is unable to work for any reason, the family's survival will depend on the resourcefulness and resilience of almost every family member.

This is the Montreal in which Marie-Claire lives in the "dark spring" of 1885.

Marie-Claire shivered in her thin nightgown. The kindling in the wood stove snapped. When the flame began to lick at the larger pieces of wood, Marie-Claire replaced the iron lid on top of the stove. Wouldn't Maman be pleased to wake up with the fire already lit? She was still so tired after Philippe's birth. Marie-Claire did not know just what had happened in her parents' room that day almost a week ago, but she'd heard enough to know that having a baby must be harder work even than churning butter or hauling water.

Marie-Claire crossed the cold floor to where Emilie still slept, curled beneath the grey blanket. How tempting it was to crawl back into the warm bed with her sister until the heat of the wood stove took the chill from the air. But if she wanted everything to be ready before Maman awoke, she must keep moving.

She slipped on her boots and wrapped her shawl around her shoulders before crouching beside the bed and pulling from under it the chamber pot. She carried it carefully so its contents wouldn't slosh out before she got downstairs to the privy in the lane behind their house.

Already a set of footprints in the snow led to the door of the little wooden shed. Marie-Claire could hear her neighbour grunting inside.

"Hurry up, Monsieur Flaubert. It's cold out here."

The door swung open. "Mind your tongue, you sassy little girl."

Marie-Claire scowled. She wasn't a little girl.

She was ten years old. Old enough to read and write and get up first and help Maman get the family ready for church.

She dumped her sister's nighttime urine down the hole, then lifted her nightgown and sat on the wooden seat, still warm from Monsieur Flaubert's big behind.

By the time Marie-Claire had emptied her parents' chamber pot, shaken the snow from her nightgown, hung it by the wood stove to dry, and got dressed, it was time to start breakfast. Marie-Claire put another stick of wood in the stove, poured water from the bucket into the kettle and set it on top. She cut five slices of bread from the loaf, ready to make toast—one piece for Emilie, one for Maman, two for Papa, and one for herself. Her baby brother was too little yet for more than the milk and water in his bottles, and her older brother had gone away with the army to help with a fight in the west. A fight with a man whose name—Louis—was the same as his own.

From the bedroom came a sudden cry. Papa

appeared in the doorway holding Philippe awkwardly in his arms.

"Here, Marie-Claire, you take him. Maman is getting dressed and I have to pay a visit."

Marie-Claire crooned a song to the baby as she danced him around the room. "*D'où viens-tu, bergère? D'où viens-tu?*"

"Marie-Claire," Maman said, "did you light the fire this morning? Such a helpful girl you are becoming. And look at this bread, already sliced. It will have to be thin ones for the rest of the day, though."

"I am sorry, Maman. I was not thinking of later." This being Sunday, the market, of course, would be closed.

"Never mind, *ma petite*. Let me feed Philippe while you go wake your sleepy sister. We do not want to be late for church."

Marie-Claire crooned a song to the baby as she danced him around the room. "D'où viens-tu, bergère? D'où viens-tu?"

As they did every Sunday, as they had for as long as Marie-Claire could remember, her family met her cousin Lucille's family in the road and they walked together to the big church.

Except for the church bells, the streets were quiet that morning, the usual sounds of trotting horses, sleigh bells, and people calling to each other muffled by the heavy snow that had been falling all weekend. Wading through it, the women talked about the new baby and how little he slept between feedings. The men talked about

7

how nice it was to sleep late this one day of the week when they did not have to go to work, although as a fireman Papa was sometimes called out no matter what day it was. As Emilie ran ahead with Lucille's little sister Bernadette, Marie-Claire and Lucille walked arm in arm, making plans for the future, when they would have big families of their own.

"Let's promise to live on the same street always," Lucille said.

Marie-Claire agreed. "That way we can do our laundry and take care of our children together, as my maman and yours do now."

Inside the church, the two families squeezed into their pews. The smell of wet wool and incense tickled Marie-Claire's nose in a pleasing way. The music from the organ sounded to Marie-Claire a little like crying, but it was a happy kind of crying, with her family—all except for Louis—kneeling together, elbows touching, thanking God for all their blessings. And Marie-Claire never tired of watching the hundreds of flickering candles while the priest preached the sermon and said prayers in his voice that was itself a little like music. "Please, God," he was saying, "accept today a special prayer for the well-being of our soldiers who have gone west to fight, and for an early end to the violence. Please, if it be part of your plan, bring these men home soon to their loving families."

"Oh, yes," Marie-Claire silently prayed, "please let Louis come home soon. Maman is worried about him, and Papa is worried too. I heard him say to my Oncle Henri that he does not like that Louis might have to fight against other French-speaking men. And I do miss him, dear Father, even if we do sometimes argue when he is helping me with my lessons."

Marie-Claire realized suddenly that everyone was standing. The organ was playing chords for the closing hymn. She rose quickly from her knees.

CHAPTER N.º 3

The snow continued to fall in fat flakes that clogged the streets. Going to school, Marie-Claire and Lucille carried their sisters on their backs, dumping them in huge drifts when they needed a rest.

The teacher, in her tidy black habit, a white wimple framing her stern face, scolded them in the doorway. "From the looks of your skirts, you have not been behaving as our Lord expects young ladies to behave."

"No, Sister," said Marie-Claire.

"We're sorry, Sister," said Lucille.

After school the girls thought nothing of how the Lord might expect them to behave. This was probably the last good snowfall of the season, and on the way home they ran and slid and jumped in the drifts. After checking that no adults were looking, Marie-Claire even threw a snowball at Jean-Paul, another of her cousins, who was on his way home from the boys' school.

"Let's build a snow fort," Lucille suggested.

In a great snowbank by the side of the road, Marie-Claire, Emilie, Lucille, and Bernadette dug and dug. Their fingers and toes were numb inside their thin gloves and boots, but in their dark little cave they giggled as they watched traffic go by, sleigh bells jingling from the horses' bellies as they pulled their carts and carriages through the heavy snow.

When one of the carts to go by was a fireman's hose wagon, Marie-Claire watched for the ladder wagon to follow. Where, she wondered, were the fire wagons going? Not to a house near where she lived, she hoped. So often, Papa had told her, when one house in a neighbourhood burned, so did others nearby.

But the ladder wagon did not come. Nor did a steam wagon. Perhaps the hose wagon was not on its way to a fire at all. It was odd that two firemen were riding in the wagon on top of the hoses.

A sudden unease gripped Marie-Claire. She crawled out of the snow fort into the street. The hose wagon was turning a corner—in the direction Marie-Claire lived. "Come, Emilie. We must go home. Hurry."

"Can't we play a little longer?"

"No. Come." Marie-Claire reached into the fort and yanked Emilie's sleeve.

"What is it?" Lucille said. "If you are worried your maman will be cross about your wet skirt, it is too late for that now."

"Something is wrong, Lucille. I know it."

Lucille and Bernadette ran to keep up with their cousins.

The fire wagon was parked in front of Marie-Claire's house, but the only smoke in the street came from chimneys. Marie-Claire ran up the stairs and, out of breath, pushed open the door.

The big shapes of two firemen filled the room. They were standing over Maman, who sat weeping in her chair. In Maman's hand a wooden spoon dripped gravy onto the floor.

Marie-Claire turned quickly to her sister. "You go with Lucille and Bernadette. I will come and get you later."

"What are those men doing here?" Emilie asked.

Marie-Claire pushed her sister out the door. "I will explain later."

In the cradle, Philippe was wailing. Marie-Claire picked him up to quiet him.

"Where is Papa?" She was afraid to ask, but had to know.

"Your papa is a brave man," one of the firemen said.

"I know that." Marie-Claire swallowed hard.

"But I asked you, where is he?"

"It was a very bad fire," the other fireman said, "up in Saint-Jean Baptiste village. A burning rafter fell, your papa could not get out of the way in time."

"He is dead?" Marie-Claire ran to Maman's side. "You are telling me Papa is dead!?"

"No, no, not dead. No." The fireman crouched down. Marie-Claire looked into his soot-streaked face. The smell of smoke was heavy in his woollen uniform. "But he is badly hurt. He will be in bed for some time. Your maman will need your help to take care of him."

Marie-Claire cradled Philippe in one arm. "My papa, may I see him?"

"He is sleeping," Maman said. "Don't wake him."

Marie-Claire peered into her parents' bedroom. Papa's face was soot-black. His neck and one cheek were red, blistered, and shiny where someone had applied grease. One arm, tied to a board with white bandage, lay on top of his blanket.

There were thick bandages around his shoulder, too.

How lucky they were, how lucky, that Papa had not been killed. Suddenly, in her wet clothes, Marie-Claire shivered. "Thank you, God," she whispered, "thank you. But please, if it is not too much trouble, while you are keeping Louis and the other soldiers safe out west, can you please help Papa to recover quickly?"

CHAPTER N.º 4

"*Maman, what is all this?*"

When Marie-Claire and Emilie came home
from school, Maman was usually chopping cabbage
or potatoes, stirring beans in the big pot on the
stove, or going through the oats to take out
mealworms before making porridge. Today, the
wooden table was covered with piles of cut
fabric. At a sewing machine, Maman was stitch-
ing two of them together.

"Shirts," Maman said. "At least they will be
shirts when I have finished sewing them."

"So many?" Marie-Claire asked. Papa and Louis could not wear so many in a lifetime.

"Yes. Monsieur Grenier brings me the pieces that have been cut at the factory. He will bring more when these shirts are finished. Fortunately Tante Celine was able to lend me her sewing machine."

"You are working like poor Madame Masson up the road?"

"While Papa is unable to work. Yes." Maman's foot moved up and down on the pedal to keep the needle of the sewing machine moving as she spoke. "Will you get some onions from the pantry, please, and start chopping them?"

"How is Papa?" Marie-Claire found a corner of the table away from the shirt material and began to chop.

"Careful. Hold your fingers out straight. We don't want to find bits of them in the soup." Maman snipped the ends of thread from the seam she had just sewn. "Papa is in pain. It may be some weeks before he can get back to work.

While I am taking in sewing for Monsieur Grenier, I will need your help around here even more than before. I'm afraid you will have to miss school."

Marie-Claire hated the thought of missing school. The nuns were very strict, but Marie-Claire loved the arithmetic they were teaching—multiplying and dividing, much more complicated and fun than simple adding and subtracting.

Emilie tugged on the sleeve of Marie-Claire's dress. "Can you play with me?"

"Later, when I have finished making supper." But by the time Marie-Claire had finished chopping vegetables, fetched another bucket of water from the tap in the slushy back lane, set the soup on the stove, given Philippe a bottle, and taken Papa a mug of hot tea, it was time to help Maman clear the table of sewing. Supper was already late.

"Thank you, Lord, for the food you have provided," Maman said. "This is very good, Marie-Claire."

"Thank you."

"But a little more salt next time, eh?" With her fingers she took a pinch from the salt jug and sprinkled it in her bowl. "Tomorrow," Maman said, "we will need a bigger pot of soup. Your Tante Thérèse and Oncle Henri are coming."

"For supper?"

"Yes, and to live with us for a time."

"But where will they sleep?"

"Henri will sleep in Louis's bed. Thérèse will sleep with you and Emilie."

"Can't they just come for supper and then go back to their own house?"

"I cannot earn enough sewing shirts to make up for your papa's lost wages. Having your Tante Thérèse and Oncle Henri living with us will help us make ends meet. Also, as newlyweds, they are having trouble making rent payments. This will be a good arrangement for all of us."

"Maybe," Emilie suggested, "my Tante Thérèse can cook for us and take care of Philippe while you sew, so Marie-Claire can keep going to school."

"Thérèse cleans rooms at the hotel all day," Maman said, "while Henri works at the foundry. I'm sorry, Marie-Claire, if there was another way to manage . . ."

Some girls, Marie-Claire knew, were sent to live at the orphanage while their parents were having a difficult time. She would certainly rather give up school than do that. It was bad enough that Louis had to be away, but to be apart from her parents and from Emilie and Philippe, too? It was unthinkable.

Marie-Claire licked the last drip of soup from her spoon and brought the metal dishpan to the table. She lifted the square lid at the end of the wood stove.

"Oh, Maman. After I built up the fire, I forgot to fill the well with water."

"Don't worry," Maman said. "Let's just wash the dishes in cold water tonight. We're all tired." With grey circles under her eyes and her hair coming undone from its bun, Maman looked especially tired.

For a long time in the middle of the night, Maman was up with Philippe, trying to stop his crying. From her bed, Marie-Claire watched in the candlelight as Maman rocked him. She hoped he was all right. Their last baby, Pierre, had died when he was just a little older than Philippe. And the mess in Philippe's diapers lately was looking an awful lot like Pierre's did.

Marie-Claire slipped from beneath the blanket and knelt beside her bed for the second time that night. "Please, God," she whispered, "I love this baby so much. Please don't let Philippe die."

CHAPTER N⁰ 5

The streets were slushy and muddy, and as Marie-Claire hurried along, she had to jump over many large puddles. Ice on the river groaned. People were saying that if it jammed this year at breakup, there would surely be flooding.

With every puddle she jumped, Marie-Claire recited another multiplication fact. "Six times three is eighteen." During her absence from school she did not want to forget all she had learned. "Seven times four is twenty-eight."

She called "*Bonjour*" to the organ grinder on

the corner but could not stop today to talk. She had to fetch, before the store closed, more of the medicine that would stop Papa from crying out in his sleep. He got out of bed in the daytime now and did his best to be cheerful, but Marie-Claire could see in the tight muscles of his face that it took great effort.

In the square, not far from where she would buy the medicine, huge but shrinking lumps of ice were all that remained of the wonderful ice palace that had stood there during the winter carnival. What a sight it had been—the glassy walls glistening in the sun like giant diamonds, flags of France and England flapping snappily in the cold wind. Many times Marie-Claire and Lucille had admired the palace till their toes grew numb.

"Imagine being a servant in such a castle," Lucille had said.

"If you are going to imagine," Marie-Claire had answered, "why not imagine being the Snow Queen?"

How long ago that seemed now. How much

easier life had been then—before Louis went away, before Papa's accident, before Maman started sewing for Monsieur Grenier and Philippe was still safe inside her, when there was time for going to school and playing with Emilie and Lucille. Except for church on Sundays and the times Lucille came around with Tante Celine when she brought extra bread or soup, the girls had hardly seen each other at all since Papa's accident.

With the bottle of medicine now in her pocket, Marie-Claire longed to get on the streetcar, to sit on one of the wooden benches in the covered cart and let the horses pull her tired body closer to her home. But even with the wages of her aunt and uncle coming into the house, there were no extra nickels for streetcar fare. She would just have to pick her way as best she could around the garbage appearing in disgusting piles with the melting of the snow.

"It's terrible," her Tante Thérèse was saying when Marie-Claire entered the house, shaking mud from her skirt. "Just terrible. Their arms were swollen hard like big red balloons. And the fevers! You can't tell me this is better than smallpox."

"Whose arms?" Marie-Claire asked. "What fevers?"

"Marie-Claire, you're interrupting," Maman said, re-threading the needle on the sewing machine.

"It's all right, Hélène. At the orphanage—I heard about this at the hotel today, one of the cleaners there does some work for the nuns, too—at the orphanage, doctors came to give the children a needle. They say it's to keep them from getting *la picotte*, but you should see them. It's terrible. Me, I'd rather be sick than go through what those poor children . . ." Thérèse shook her head. "Apparently, a few people in the city are sick with smallpox and the doctors say it could spread. Sure it's bad, those ugly spots you get, but what's a few people? Do we know anyone who has it? No. What I know is, those needles they want to give are horrible."

"Will I have to get a needle, Maman?"

"Of course not. Be a dear now and see if Papa wants some of his medicine."

CHAPTER N.º 6

Huge slabs of ice cracked and heaved along the banks of the river. Warm winds rippled the surface of puddles, growing larger by the hour, in the streets and back lanes.

From his chair at the end of the table, where he was now able to sit comfortably for some hours, Papa said, "The noise of that river breaking up reminds me of artillery fire."

Marie-Claire placed a bowl of beans in front of him. "When I was down there yesterday, I could hear the river humming. *Humming*, Papa, like it is something alive."

"It speaks, it moves, it rises and falls—who knows, maybe it *is* alive."

When the river flooded, its waters flowed over the harbour wall. They flowed on through the lower streets of the city where Marie-Claire and her family lived. The river water mixed with the filthy water draining down from the mountain. Water continued to rise till it covered sidewalks and seeped under doors.

Looking out the window, Papa said, "The family downstairs will be in it up to their ankles. We must invite them to come up here until the flooding recedes."

Marie-Claire's already crowded home became even more crowded as the grateful Flauberts dripped in carrying blankets and food. Monsieur Flaubert brought his fiddle, too. After supper that night the families sang and laughed together until Papa said, "I must get to bed."

Above the sound of Monsieur Flaubert's snoring, Marie-Claire heard Papa cry out sharply in his sleep, then Maman lighting a candle and rustling around for his medicine. "I am getting better," Papa whispered. "It is only at night . . ." Beside Marie-Claire her Tante Thérèse rolled over and mumbled something in her sleep. Emilie's hand reached up and stroked Marie-Claire's cheek.

On the floor, Monsieur Flaubert stopped snoring. His little boy said, "Is it morning yet?"

"Not yet, *chéri*," Madame Flaubert whispered. "Go back to sleep."

Marie-Claire closed her eyes. "Thank you, God, for keeping us all safe here, but please can you stop the flood by morning? Our house is really not big enough for all these extra people."

Outside, something thumped against the house. A chunk of wood maybe? Another dead cow? Was the spring flooding worse this year than last? Was God angry at the people of Montreal for something they had done or not done?

The next day, Marie-Claire hauled in extra buckets of water and boiled Philippe's diapers without complaining. She kept Emilie and the Flauberts' little boy entertained with stories. Muddy water continued to lap against the sides of the house. Except to visit the privy and the community tap, awash in flood water, no one ventured out.

By lunchtime they had eaten all the bread. Tante Thérèse suggested that she and Madame Flaubert could make some biscuits. Maman said, "Don't use any milk in them, please. Philippe will need what we have for his next bottle. The last one I gave him was mostly water."

Marie-Claire opened the window and leaned out. Could she see, above the muddy water, a wet line on the walls of the houses across the street? How much farther did the water have to fall before they could go out? She was about to close the window when, standing on some kind of raft, her cousin Jean-Paul appeared.

"Marie-Claire," he shouted, "is there anything I can bring your family?"

"Where did you get your raft?"

"The sidewalk on my street is busting up. I tied a couple of boards together, and *voilà!* Using another board for a paddle, I can go anywhere."

"Can you bring us some milk, Jean-Paul, for the baby?" She tossed down an earthenware bottle with some money in the bottom, which Jean-Paul caught neatly.

In twenty minutes he returned and tossed the bottle back up to the window. "Good catch, Marie-Claire," he said.

CHAPTER N°7

Finally, several days later, the Flaubert family returned home.

"Maman, I wish my Tante Thérèse and Oncle Henri would go home too." They were both out at work, so Marie-Claire could speak freely as she scraped the scales from the fish she was preparing for supper.

"We are lucky to have them here." Maman guided two pieces of material under the up-and-down needle of the sewing machine. "Without their help, I don't know what we would do while Papa is unable to work."

"I could go to work at the tobacco factory," Marie-Claire suggested. "Josephine has a job there."

"Anyone who would hire such a young girl I do not want you working for. Besides, if you went away to work, who would help me here?"

"I can help you, Maman," Emilie said, rocking Philippe's cradle in the corner.

Maman was right, of course. Emilie could clean boots and help a little with the baby, but she could not do the work that was now Marie-Claire's—shopping, preparing meals for the family, hauling water for cooking, and cleaning and laundry. So many diapers she boiled every day. Also, even if she could take a paying job, as a child her wage would be very small.

"Maybe if I help you more," Marie-Claire said as she dumped fish guts into the slop bucket, "you can make even more shirts, and we won't need my Oncle Henri and Tante Thérèse any more."

Maman stopped the whirring machine. "Why do you want them to leave, Marie-Claire? I thought you liked them."

"I do. But beside me in bed my Tante Thérèse does not always smell very nice. And why does my Oncle Henri have to shout all the time? I am sure the Flauberts downstairs can hear every word he says."

"I'm afraid," Maman said, "that your Oncle Henri is losing his hearing. He does not realize he speaks so loudly."

"Losing his hearing? He is not much older than Louis, is he?"

"All the clanging and banging of machinery at the foundry twelve hours a day, six days a week— it is a wonder Henri can hear at all after two years working there."

Marie-Claire nodded. But still, she longed to have things at home back as they should be.

Before going to the market the next day, Marie-Claire slipped into the church to sit by herself in the quiet and remember what it had been like before the burning rafter crashed down on Papa. Sunlight shone in through the stained-glass windows.

"Please, God, help me be more patient with our crowded house, and don't let my Oncle Henri get any more deaf than he already is. Please can you try to mend Papa's shoulder a little faster? And please don't let my dear Lucille forget we are friends at this time when I cannot go to school or play with her." Afraid that asking so much would make her appear ungrateful, Marie-Claire added, "Thank you for keeping Philippe alive, even if he is still so sick, and thank you for getting Maman to say I don't have to get the awful needle that did bad things to the arms of the children at the orphanage."

On Sunday, with the candles flickering and the organ playing its sad but everything-will-be-all-right music, Marie-Claire bowed her head and said the same prayer. During the sermon, she leaned slightly forward and glanced along the pew to where Lucille sat, with her back straight and her hands folded in her lap. Lucille must have felt her friend's eyes upon her because she turned then toward Marie-Claire and smiled warmly.

"Let us pray," the priest said. He prayed that members of the congregation should choose the correct path, be grateful for their blessings, and honour God in their daily words and deeds. He prayed that the troops from Montreal should not be sent into the thick of the fighting in the west.

Marie-Claire was shocked to realize she had forgotten her big brother in her personal prayers. "Dear God," she quickly prayed, "forgive me for being selfish, please, and keep our Louis safe."

CHAPTER N°. 8

Day by day, as summer approached, the smell in the streets got worse. Barrels of manure overflowed into big puddles in laneways. Dead rats sprawled among rotting heaps of vegetable scraps, fish, eggs, and bones. One morning, between her home and the market, Marie-Claire counted six of them—and two dead pigs so disgustingly decayed that they must have been drowned in the floods earlier in the spring.

Around the market, where there were no privies at all, and where sewer drains were clogged with everything the butchers and other stall-keepers tossed out, Marie-Claire twice had to grasp her stomach and will its contents not to come up. With every step she took, something squished underfoot.

As she did the shopping, Marie-Claire did her best to remember all that Maman had taught her. Don't let anyone sell you meat that has maggots in it. The apple woman with the scar on her cheek has the nicest apples. Watch that the man selling flour does not put his finger on the scale. Don't ever pay for anything the first price you are given.

Marie-Claire roamed among barrels and baskets and carts, jostling against the other girls and women out to shop and catch up on the latest news and gossip.

"I hear the city hired a new scavenging company, cheaper than the old one, but are they doing *anything* to clean the streets?"

"He's bringing little enough money into that house and then he drinks most of it away."

"Can't you just smell the disease in all this filth? No wonder we've got smallpox in this city."

"But what would you have her do, Claudette?"

"Oh, I heard it is all over. A few cases there were, that is all."

"I hope so. A dreadful illness it is. If it doesn't kill you, its spots can leave you scarred for life."

"If you do get it, don't let the black wagon take you. In hospital you are almost sure to die."

With a cabbage, some carrots, and a few potatoes in her basket, Marie-Claire headed to a stall where chickens hung by their feet.

"How much for that one?" she asked. When the vendor reached up, she said, "I'm here to buy meat, not skin and bones. I was asking about the next one over."

The vendor placed the chicken on his scale. "Forty-five cents."

Marie-Claire wished she had enough money in her pocket to just pay it. She hated arguing for a better price. But Maman had said, "They don't expect you to pay what they ask." And it wasn't really arguing, it was bargaining.

Marie-Claire took a deep breath. "Not worth it," she said, and as Maman had taught her, she began to walk away. She hoped the next farmer would not be charging even more for his chickens.

"All right then, forty-one cents. Six cents off."

Marie-Claire turned back. "Six cents off makes thirty-nine." Holding herself tall, her heart pounding in her chest, she said, "I will pay you thirty-six."

The vendor handed Marie-Claire the chicken. "I am going to be a poor man at this rate."

"*Merci, monsieur,* thank you."

The man laughed as she headed off to buy a loaf of bread and a bag of beans.

With a few cents left in her pocket, Marie-Claire went to a stall inside the long marketplace and bought some beef bones. Sometimes a little broth in Philippe's bottle helped him sleep a little longer before waking again with his awful little cry.

CHAPTER N⁰ 9

Philippe stopped making the foul messes in his diaper. It seemed he was getting better. But one morning, after emptying the chamber pots, Marie-Claire realized that the house was oddly quiet. She ran to her parents' bedroom.

"I am sorry," Maman said. "Philippe passed away in the night. He was not strong enough."

"Why, Maman? Why wasn't he strong enough?" Tears streamed down Marie-Claire's cheeks.

Maman stared into the cradle. "It is God's way."

"But two babies in one family? It is not fair!"

Maman's lips almost disappeared in a thin line. "It is God's way."

Marie-Claire's bones felt heavy, but she tried to work fast that day so she could go to meet Lucille when she came out of school. She had to talk to someone who would understand how sad she felt. Maman seemed to have no heart left in her at all.

"But your maman is right," Lucille said. "It is not ours to question why God chooses those he does. And there are many babies God lets us keep for just a short while."

"That is all very easy for you to say. You have not had two babies die at your house before they had even one birthday."

"It is a shame your maman must spend so many hours sewing . . ."

"Are you saying it is Maman's *fault* that Philippe died? Or *mine*?! Lucille, you horrid witch! How can you be so cruel? You are as cruel as . . . as God!"

Marie-Claire hurried so she could meet Lucille after school. She had to talk to someone who would understand how sad she felt.

"Marie-Claire! You will be punished for saying such a thing. You had better hurry now to church and beg forgiveness."

"I will not! And I will never speak to you again! I wish instead of Philippe it was *you* who was dead!"

Throngs of people packed the streets singing hymns. No one wanted to miss the parade for La Fête Dieu, winding its way, under golden banners and a hot sun, to Notre Dame. As crowds flocked into the vast church with twin towers, people agreed that this had been the grandest procession yet.

For Marie-Claire it was not. It was the only spring celebration of earthly blessings she had ever attended without Lucille.

In spite of the warm stuffiness of the church,

Emilie leaned against Marie-Claire in the crowded pew. Marie-Claire wrapped an arm around her little sister.

"Are you sad too?" she asked.

Emilie nodded. "Philippe never got to see a festival," she whispered.

"I know." If only Lucille understood.

All around, people's heads were bowed in prayer. Marie-Claire bowed her head too, but once again, like every day since Philippe's death, prayers would not come.

Coming out of the church, Marie-Claire and Lucille avoided each other's eyes, but Marie-Claire noticed how flushed her cousin's face was. Had it been that hot inside, or was Lucille ashamed of the cruel things she had said? Good. She should be. Or maybe she had a bad fever. That would be fine too.

Marie-Claire took Emilie's hand and Maman's arm and, without a word to Lucille, stepped into the street. Such mean thoughts she could not stop herself thinking. Perhaps she was herself a bad person—fighting with her best friend, being glad if she had a fever. Being unable to think of something to thank God for was bad too, and the feeling she had that asking him for anything was pointless, because hadn't he let Philippe die, and wasn't Louis still out west, and wasn't Papa still unable to go back to work at the fire station?

Back home Emilie played quietly with her clothespin doll. Papa and Oncle Henri smoked their pipes while Tante Thérèse plucked a chicken and Maman chopped carrots. Maman never did her sewing on Sundays.

The pieces of fabric waiting to be sewn on Monday sat piled in the corner. Some of the pieces were quite small. About the right size, Marie-Claire thought, for a little dress for Emilie's naked doll.

Not wanting to interrupt the conversation Maman and her Tante Thérèse were having, she took one of the smallest pieces of fabric from the pile, threaded a needle and, wrapping the material around the neck of Emilie's doll, sewed her a dress. It was just a simple little dress, gathered around the neck and stitched down the back, but Emilie beamed.

Marie-Claire smiled. Maybe she wasn't such a bad person after all.

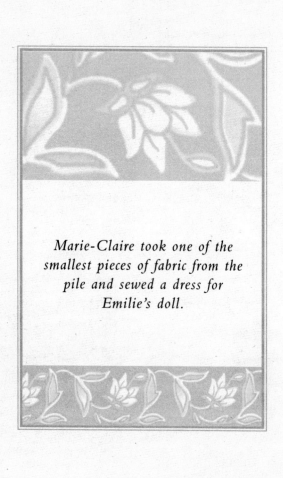

*Marie-Claire took one of the
smallest pieces of fabric from the
pile and sewed a dress for
Emilie's doll.*

CHAPTER Nº 11

The bishop was dead. Gathered round the table the day after La Fête Dieu, Marie-Claire's parents could talk of nothing else.

"We have so much because of him. Schools and hospitals, organizations to help the poor."

"Not to mention all the new churches."

"So beautiful . . ."

"He was a good man."

"A fine bishop."

But is death such a sad thing, Marie-Claire wondered, when someone is so old? There had been less talk about little Philippe, yet how much more her heart ached at his passing.

So much was the bishop loved that the procession for his funeral was even bigger than the parade for La Fête Dieu. Marie-Claire could hardly believe the hundreds of carriages and thousands of people in the streets. Among the faces were several, she noticed, covered in spots. Could these people have the smallpox her aunt and women in the market had spoken of? Were there now more than just a few cases of it in the city? Marie-Claire had only a moment to wonder before she was caught up again in the spectacle of bands, horses and carriages, bishops, police, students, nuns, and important men, all clutching prayer books or rosaries as they marched by.

Never before, Marie-Claire was sure, could the church have been so packed. Even when all the pews were filled, people continued to pour in the doors. From every pillar hung black-and-orange banners, like those hanging on many of the buildings outside.

Marie-Claire snuggled in close to Papa. It was wonderful to have him back at church. He had been exercising his arm and shoulder a lot and was able to sit and even stand for long periods now without having to go and lie down.

"A person would have to be dead himself," Papa said, "not to attend the funeral for such a great bishop as Ignace Bourget."

The chanting of the choir of hundreds echoed throughout the vast cathedral and hummed right through Marie-Claire's body. It put something back inside her, somehow, that had been missing. She bowed her head and thanked God at length for his many blessings, even for letting them have Philippe for a while. She thanked God for giving her back her ability to pray.

When she finished praying, she looked around for Lucille. She must be here today. Where was she? Marie-Claire wanted to go to her and tell her she forgave her the awful things she'd said and apologize for her own hurtful words. She found Lucille a few rows behind, between her parents, her head bowed. She would speak to her when the service was over.

When Lucille looked up, Marie-Claire's heart dropped into her stomach. Angry red spots covered Lucille's face. Some of the spots oozed shiny pus.

Smallpox? It must be. But had her Tante Thérèse or someone not said that people could die of this ugly thing? *Lucille, I wish you were dead.* That was what she, Marie-Claire, had said.

"Oh, dear God, please, no!"

*When Lucille looked up,
Marie-Claire's heart dropped into
her stomach. Angry red spots
covered Lucille's face. It had
to be smallpox.*

CHAPTER N.º 12

"*Marie-Claire, what is this?*" Maman's voice cut like an axe into Marie-Claire's absent-minded stirring of the soup. "Did you do this?"

Maman held up Emilie's little doll, still proudly wearing the dress Marie-Claire had made. Maman's face was pulled into an angry scowl, angrier than Marie-Claire had ever before seen.

"I did, Maman. Emilie was so sad, I wanted to do something to make her feel a little better."

"And so you took something of mine without asking?"

"You were busy. It was just a little piece. I—"

"A whole shirt ruined because of *just a little piece*. You foolish, foolish child! Do you think Monsieur Grenier will pay me for a shirt that is missing a cuff?" Maman shouted. "No! He will charge me a fine for the ruined shirt! And after all the work I have done!"

"I am sorry, Maman, I truly am. I didn't know."

"As if things were not difficult enough!"

"I know, I know, I said I am sorry! What else can I do?!" Without waiting for an answer Marie-Claire ran from the house.

It wasn't fair. All she took was one little cuff! Was it her fault Maman worked for such a mean boss? Was that any reason to be so mean herself? It wasn't fair at all, when Marie-Claire worked so hard to cook, clean, take care of Emilie, do shopping and laundry, while all Maman did was sit around sewing shirts.

A hot, damp breeze blew off the river.

Of course, that wasn't true. Maman worked hard too. Marie-Claire had often seen her wince as she tried to stretch her back after so many hours bent over the sewing machine. And now, because of her awful daughter, Maman would not get all the money she had earned.

Everything, it seemed, was because of her, Marie-Claire. Maman being upset, and the family being short of money. The fact that her cousin Lucille was sick and dying was her fault too. Marie-Claire ran and ran, but she could not get away from herself.

At the market, with a stitch in her side and sweat pouring down her forehead, she trudged aimlessly from stall to stall. Tonight before bed she would pray for a good long time. She would ask God to help her be a better person. In the meantime—yes, she had a little change in her pocket left over from the trip to market when she had got such a good bargain on a block of cheese. Was it enough to buy a loaf of the bread Maman especially liked but bought only for special occasions? It would not make up for the ruined shirt, and maybe Maman would be angry if she spent money on bread unnecessarily, but Marie-Claire wanted so much to make some kind of peace offering.

Luck was with her. The bread was a day old and she got it at a very good price. Quickly she made her way toward home, her dress sticking to her back.

"Marie-Claire! Come!" Jean-Paul shouted. "On your street! The black wagon!"

Marie-Claire hugged the loaf of bread she had bought and ran behind Jean-Paul to the end of the dirt lane where she lived. Outside Lucille's house was parked the black wagon. Policemen were shouting at Lucille's father.

"She must go!"

"No. Please!" Lucille's father begged. "We can take good care of her at home." Behind him cowered Lucille, tears streaming down her spotty face.

Marie-Claire had heard that people with *la picotte* were sometimes forced to go in the black wagon to the hospital, but her best friend? "This is not possible," she whispered. She must go to Lucille right now and beg her forgiveness. She must pray to God to correct this awful mistake.

But before she could get near Lucille, the doors of the black wagon, with Lucille inside, slammed shut.

CHAPTER N.º 13

Throughout all the singing and speeches on Saint-Jean Baptiste Day celebrating the survival of the French-Canadian people, Marie-Claire could think of and hope for the survival of just one of them. "Lucille, Lucille, you must get well."

So that her Tante Celine could go and visit at the hospital, Marie-Claire offered to take care of Lucille's little sister. She took Bernadette and Emilie down to the river to watch the men in shirt sleeves loading big sacks, barrels, and boxes onto the huge ships. When the girls tired of that,

Marie-Claire tied a rope to a lamppost and turned it and turned it till finally the girls grew tired of skipping, too. At home, she worked fast and hard as if, if she could just be good enough, it would help ensure Lucille's recovery. "And please, God," she prayed, "can you try to prevent the spots from leaving permanent scars? Lucille has such a pretty face."

When, two weeks later, Marie-Claire heard that Lucille was home, she whooped with joy.

"Please, Maman, may I go and see her?"

"Of course. Go. You have been working your fingers to the bone here. You'll be an old woman before you're twelve years old at the rate you've been going. Go now. I'm sure Lucille will be pleased to see you."

Will she? As Marie-Claire passed the scavengers shovelling slimy garbage into wagons, she wondered.

"Come in, Marie-Claire, come in." Her Tante Celine was up to her elbows in flour. "Lucille is just picking over the oatmeal for me. It's so good to have her home again."

Lucille's head was bent over a sack on a chair in front of her. With her fingers she gently sifted the oats, pausing occasionally to toss a mealworm into the fire.

As if sensing something between the girls, Tante Celine suddenly wiped her hands on her apron, said, "I just remembered something I must be doing," and left them alone.

"Lucille, I came to apologize," Marie-Claire said quickly. "I am sorry for what I said." When Lucille said nothing, Marie-Claire went on. "I cannot stand it when we argue. I said things I did not mean and I was so afraid—oh, Lucille, you don't know how afraid I have been. When you went to hospital I thought you would die and it would be all my fault."

"Do you really think you are as powerful as all that?" Lucille looked up at Marie-Claire for the first time. Faded spots still marked her forehead and one cheek. "And do you honestly think you were more frightened than I?"

"No. Of course not. No. But please, Lucille ..." Marie-Claire pulled a chair over beside her cousin and sat down. "Can you please try to find it in your heart to forgive me?"

"Marie-Claire, can you imagine being in hospital, your throat parched and your ugly skin burning up and no one comes for hours with a glass of water or a cool cloth? Can you imagine lying there and beside you in the next bed a girl has died and you call for the nuns to come, but there are so many patients, who knows when they will?"

Marie-Claire let her tears drop into her lap. After all Lucille had been through, it was no wonder she could not forgive her.

"But it is not your fault I got smallpox," Lucille continued. "It is not your fault I went to hospital. There are so many people in the city with the disease now, they are saying it is an epidemic. And of course . . ." Lucille smiled then, "of course I *must* forgive you. I could not bear it either when we were not speaking."

Marie-Claire pushed the oatmeal bag out of

the way, threw her arms around her cousin, and kissed her on both cheeks. Her face must have betrayed what suddenly occurred to her, because Lucille laughed and said, "Don't worry. They would not have sent me home if I were still contagious."

"To be honest, Lucille, I would be more worried if we could not be friends again than I ever could be about getting sick."

"We *are* friends again." Lucille grabbed Marie-Claire's hands and squeezed. "We are friends now, and we will be friends forever."

CHAPTER Nº 14

Papa stood in the middle of the room wearing only an undershirt and trousers. In each hand he held an iron pot. With his arms stretched to either side, he slowly lifted the pots up and over his head. Slowly he lowered them again to his sides.

"Josèph, it is wonderful how well you are getting back your strength," Maman said, "but isn't that enough for today?"

"Nonsense," Papa said. "Put some potatoes in these pots so I can work these muscles harder."

"I'll work those muscles for you," Oncle Henri suggested, rolling up his sleeves. "Come on, Josèph. How about it?"

Papa set down the pots and faced Oncle Henri across the table. "Ready?"

Elbows braced on the table, the men locked hands.

"Go."

Each man tried to push the other's hand down flat to the table. Blood vessels stood out on the backs of their clenched fists. Raised knots of muscles in their arms and across their shoulders quivered. Marie-Claire clenched her own fists, as if doing so would add to Papa's strength.

After a long minute, sweat shone on Papa's face, his arm began to tremble, and Oncle Henri was able to push Papa's hand a little closer to the table. Grunting, Papa pushed back. When the two clenched hands were again upright, Marie-Claire and Emilie cheered. Oncle Henri eventually got Papa's arm down to the table, but still the girls cheered. So much stronger Papa was getting.

In time he was strong enough to carry hoses, buckets of water, even another man if necessary. The day he returned to work, Marie-Claire put extra chunks of ham in his beans and packed an extra-thick slice of bread and butter in his lunch box.

When Monsieur Grenier came to pick up Mama's shirts and bring her more pieces to sew, Mama said, "Bring me only half this number next week. My husband is back at work now. And I must get back to my work here at home so my daughter can get back to school."

At the end of the room, where she was scrubbing the floor, Marie-Claire smiled.

That night, after the family had given thanks for the food they were about to eat, Oncle Henri announced in his big voice, "Thérèse and I will soon be leaving you."

"Why?" Maman asked.

"Where will you go?"

"You don't need us here any more," Thérèse said, "and I heard at the hotel that the men we sent out west are on their way home. Riel has fled, and the rebellion is over."

Marie-Claire dropped her fork to her plate. "Our Louis is coming home?"

"If it be God's will," Maman said, her voice full of hope.

"Oh, please, God, let it be so," Marie-Claire exclaimed. "But, my Tante Thérèse, do you and my Oncle Henri have to go? We can make room here for everyone."

Maman smiled, then looked to Thérèse and Henri. "Perhaps your aunt and uncle have other reasons to be finding a home of their own?"

"We are going to go to Toronto," Oncle Henri said. "I hear they pay men a decent wage there."

"But, Henri, you will not find many French people in Toronto," Papa said.

"My English is pretty good," Henri said. "We will be all right."

The festive mood at the table seemed broken by this news. Everyone was chewing quietly when Tante Thérèse spoke again. "Also, when winter comes, our household will have an additional little member."

"We are getting a dog?" Oncle Henri teased. "You didn't tell me!"

Tante Thérèse laughed. "If Henri finds a good enough job, we will all be able to come on the train to visit you here at Christmas."

Such a long time away Christmas seemed now, with the suffocating heat of summer wrapped tight round them.

"Let us give thanks," Papa said, "for your good fortune."

"And for the hope that Louis may be home soon," Marie-Claire added.

"And for Josèph's recovery," said Maman.

"For all the good things in life," Oncle Henri shouted, "let us say *merci infiniment!*"

Together everyone at the table said, "Amen."

ACKNOWLEDGEMENTS

I WOULD LIKE TO THANK THE FOLLOWING FOR THE PARTS THEY PLAYED in the development of this project: my agent, Leona Trainer, for her confidence in me, for bringing to me the opportunity to contribute to the Our Canadian Girl series, and for her supportive input; my partner, Peter Carver, for his support also and for his patience during the period when I seemed to think of little but Montreal history, smallpox, and Marie-Claire's life; my editor, Barbara Berson, for developing the series and doing with *Dark Spring* what good editors do; Cindy Kantor, who brought the idea for the series to Penguin; Barbara Greenwood, Gillian O'Reilly, Bill Freeman, and Maria Varvarikos for suggesting possible resources; Fred and Eunice Tees, and Marie Louise Gay and David Homel, for their special welcomes in Montreal; Suzanne Morin at the McCord Museum in Montreal for the time she took with my many questions; Victor Fleischer and Raymond Follows at the Musée des Pompiers Auxiliares for their time and interest in this project; le Centre d'Histoire de Montreal, le Musée du Fier Monde, la Bibliothèque Nationale du Québec, le Chateau Ramezay, le Musée de Marguerite Bourgeois, le Musée d'Hospitaliers de l'Hotel Dieu, Westmount Library in Montreal, and all the Montrealers who spoke French during my time in their city; the Toronto Public Library, and especially the staff at North York Central; Michael Bliss, Bettina Bradbury, Herbert Ames, and Edgar Collard, for their books and columns that were especially helpful in conducting my research; and my writing group, Lena Coakley, Hadley Dyer, Wendy Lewis, and Paula Wing, whose feedback on the manuscript was, as always, invaluable.

Dear Reader,

Did you enjoy reading this Our Canadian Girl adventure? Write us and tell us what you think! We'd love to hear about your favourite parts, which characters you like best, and even whom else you'd like to see stories about. Maybe you'd like to read an adventure with one of Our Canadian Girls that happened in your hometown—fifty, a hundred years ago or more!

Send your letters to:

Our Canadian Girl
c/o Penguin Canada
10 Alcorn Avenue, Suite 300
Toronto, ON M4V 3B2

Be sure to check your bookstore for more books in the Our Canadian Girl series. There are some ready for you right now, and more are on their way.

We look forward to hearing from you!

Sincerely,
Barbara Berson
PENGUIN BOOKS CANADA

P.S. Don't forget to visit us online at www.ourcanadiangirl.ca—there are some other girls you should meet!

Canada's

1608
Samuel de Champlain establishes the first fortified trading post at Quebec.

1759
The British defeat the French in the Battle of the Plains of Abraham.

1812
The United States declares war against Canada.

1845
The expedition of Sir John Franklin to the Arctic ends when the ship is frozen in the pack ice; the fate of its crew remains a mystery.

1869
Louis Riel leads his Métis followers in the Red River Rebellion.

1871
British Columbia joins Canada.

1755
The British expel the entire French population of Acadia (today's Maritime provinces), sending them into exile.

1776
The 13 Colonies revolt against Britain, and the Loyalists flee to Canada.

1837
Calling for responsible government, the Patriotes, following Louis-Joseph Papineau, rebel in Lower Canada; William Lyon Mackenzie leads the uprising in Upper Canada.

1867
New Brunswick, Nova Scotia and the United Province of Canada come together in Confederation to form the Dominion of Canada.

1870
Manitoba joins Canada. The Northwest Territories become an official territory of Canada.

1783
Rachel

Timeline

1885
At Craigellachie, British Columbia, the last spike is driven to complete the building of the Canadian Pacific Railway.

1898
The Yukon Territory becomes an official territory of Canada.

1914
Britain declares war on Germany, and Canada, because of its ties to Britain, is at war too.

1918
As a result of the Wartime Elections Act, the women of Canada are given the right to vote in federal elections.

1945
World War II ends conclusively with the dropping of atomic bombs on Hiroshima and Nagasaki.

1873
Prince Edward Island joins Canada.

1896
Gold is discovered on Bonanza Creek, a tributary of the Klondike River.

1905
Alberta and Saskatchewan join Canada.

1917
In the Halifax harbour, two ships collide, causing an explosion that leaves more than 1,600 dead and 9,000 injured.

1939
Canada declares war on Germany seven days after war is declared by Britain and France.

1949
Newfoundland, under the leadership of Joey Smallwood, joins Canada.

1896
Emily

1885
Marie-Claire

1917
Penelope

Don't miss your chance to meet all the girls in the Our Canadian Girl series...

The year is 1917. Penny and her little sisters, Emily and Maggie, live with their father in a small house in Halifax. On the morning of December 6, Penny's father is at work, leaving Penny to get her sisters ready for the day. It is then that a catastrophic explosion rocks Halifax.

It's 1896 and Emily lives a middle-class life in Victoria, B.C., with her parents and two little sisters. She becomes friends with Hing, the family's Chinese servant and, through that relationship, discovers the secret world of Victoria's Chinatown.

Ten-year-old Rachel arrives in northern Nova Scotia in 1783 with her mother, where they reunite with Rachel's stepfather after escaping slavery in South Carolina. Their joy at gaining freedom in a safe new home is dashed when they arrive, for the land they are given is barren and they don't have enough to eat. How will they survive?

Watch for more Canadian girls in 2002...

Penguin Books Canada Ltd. • www.ourcanadiangirl.ca

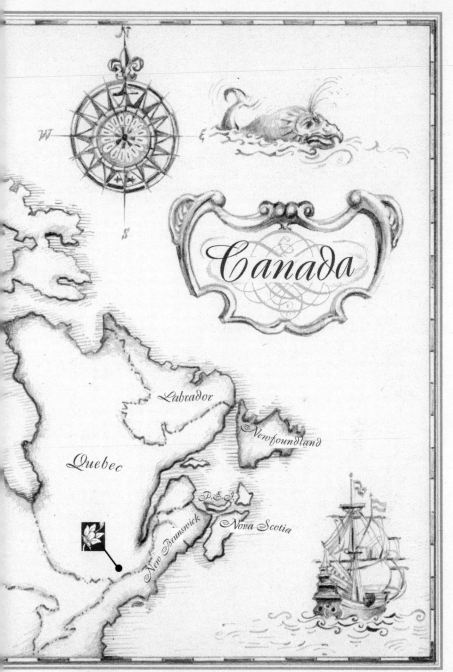

Canada

Labrador

Newfoundland

Quebec

P.E.I.

New Brunswick

Nova Scotia

 Marks the location of the story

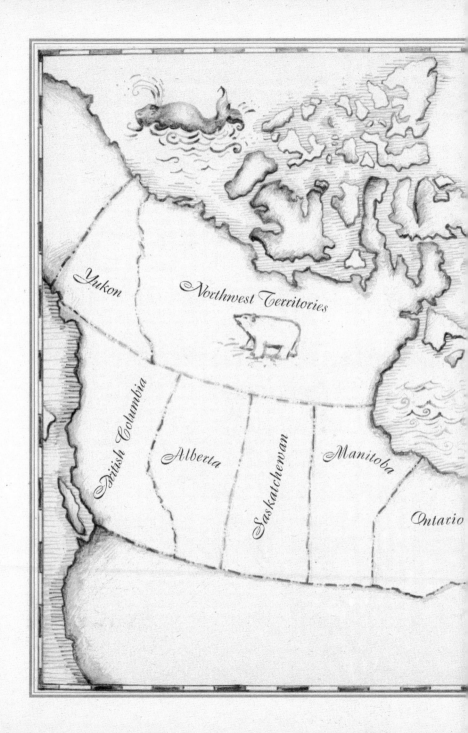